My Wonderful Aunt
Story Five

Did I ever mention
my wonderful aunt?
She wouldn't say, "No!"
and she wouldn't say, "Can't!"

She lived in a burrow
dug into the ground.
When she wanted to hide,
she could never be found.

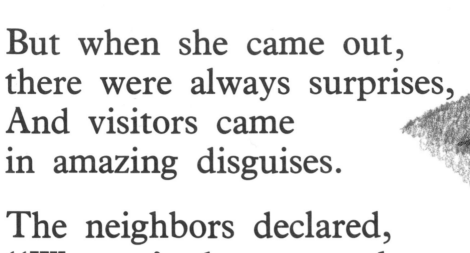

But when she came out,
there were always surprises,
And visitors came
in amazing disguises.

The neighbors declared,
"We can't do our work, as
She's turning the neighborhood
into a circus.

"She looks like a clown!
She belongs on the stage!
She ought to know better,
an aunt of her age!"

5

I went by her burrow,
delivering papers,
And there was my aunt
getting up to her capers.

I went to her burrow,
delivering mail,
She was putting up posters
proclaiming a Sale.

There were posters in trees,
there was one on the wall,
Saying, "Come along, come along,
come along all!

"Bring all the odd oddments
you want to be rid of:
Old wigs, or the teapot
that you've lost the lid of,

"That cactus that needs
an affectionate home,
Umbrellas, a bird bath,
an old garden gnome.

"Oh, bring them along
on the bring-and-buy day,
And someone will love them
and take them away."

And all the neighbors
let out a great wail
And grumbled about auntie's
Bring-and-Buy Sale.

From an ad in the paper,
my auntie had found
A gorilla, who owned
an old merry-go-round,

And a band of blue budgies,
with trumpets and drums,
Who would hop around after
and pick up the crumbs.

The music was happy,
the crowd was immense,
And shoppers crammed eagerly
into the tents.

And the neighbors stood smelling
the wonderful smell
Of popcorn and peanuts
and hot dogs as well.

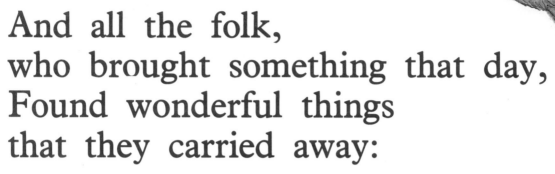

And all the folk,
who brought something that day,
Found wonderful things
that they carried away:

A necklace, a nightshirt,
a musical box,
Or one from a series
of grandfather clocks.

Then a sudden sensation!
A mew from the cat!
The gorilla smiled broadly
and took off his hat . . .

The drums they did bang,
and the trumpets did bray,
For the QUEEN came along
on the bring-and-buy day.

16

"Hello, auntie," she said.
"I have brought a small crown . . .
Not my best one,
but one that keeps making me frown.

"Now what can I buy that I'll like . .
that's the question!"
"Oh, Queen, try a hot dog,"
was auntie's suggestion.

And the neighbors,
who now saw my aunt with the queen
Eating hot dogs and mustard
and licking ice cream,

Stopped looking so scornful
and nose-in-the-air
And joined in with auntie's
great Bring-and-Buy Fair.

For the rest of the day
they all brought and they bought,
And they all said my aunt
was a wonderful sport.

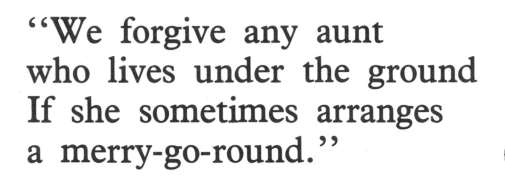

"We forgive any aunt
who lives under the ground
If she sometimes arranges
a merry-go-round."

And my aunt gave a smile
and a bit of a wink...
And so did the queen...
at least, that's what I think.